W9-CZY-333

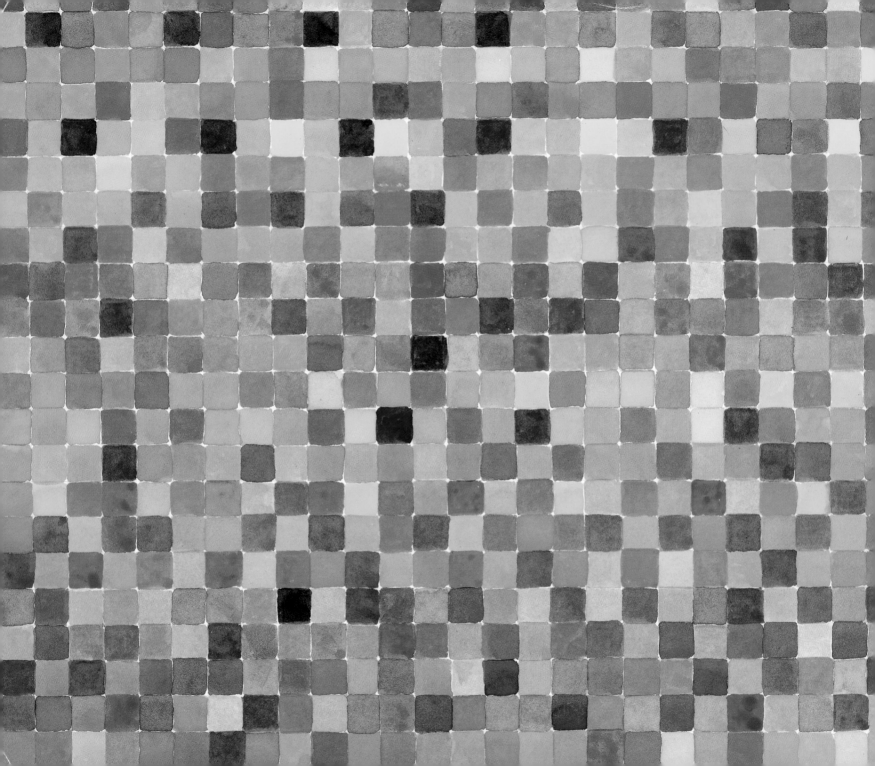

RED DAY

GREEN DAY

by **Edith Kunhardt**
pictures by **Marylin Hafner**

Greenwillow Books, New York

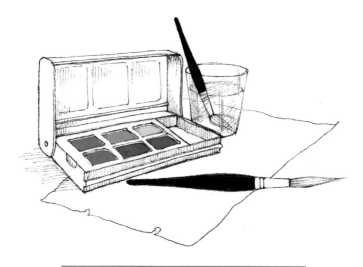

Library of Congress Cataloging-in-Publication Data
Kunhardt, Edith.
Red day, green day / by Edith Kunhardt ;
pictures by Marylin Hafner.
p.   cm.
Summary: Andrew and his classmates in Mrs. Halsey's kindergarten class learn about colors in a unique way.
ISBN 0-688-09399-X (trade).
ISBN 0-688-09400-7 (lib.)
[1. Color—Fiction.   2. Schools—Fiction.]
I. Hafner, Marylin, ill.   II. Title.
PZ7.K94905Re   1992
[E]—dc20   90-38490   CIP   AC

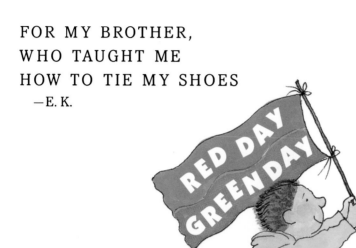

Andrew was in kindergarten.

He was in Mrs. Halsey's class.

He liked school.

Andrew liked
to hang
his coat
in his cubby.

He liked to sit in his chair.

He liked to paint
with fingerpaints
and make things
out of clay.

He liked juice

and rest

and going home.

One day Mrs. Halsey said,
"Tomorrow is Red Day.
Everyone bring something red to school.
You can show it to the class
at show-and-tell."

When it was time to go home,
Mrs. Halsey said, "Don't forget.
Tomorrow is Red Day."

Andrew got in the car.

He carried a piece of paper.

He handed the paper to his mother.

"Oh! Tomorrow is Red Day!" she exclaimed.

"What are you going to take to school for Red Day?"

When Andrew got home,
he got his red overalls
and put them on the chair
with his school clothes.
That night Andrew lay awake,
thinking about Red Day.

The next day he went to school. All of
Andrew's friends had brought something red.
Andrew told about his overalls.
"These are my favorite pants," he said.

The next week it was Orange Day.

Andrew brought some orange Jell-O.

On Yellow Day, Andrew brought
a yellow daffodil to school.

On Green Day, Andrew brought
in his favorite toy tractor.

On Blue Day, Andrew brought some blueberries.

His friends ate them all up!

On Purple Day, Andrew wore
his favorite purple socks.
And that was the end
of the color days.

The next day when Andrew went
to school, it was raining.
Andrew splashed through puddles
in the school yard.

At recess the rain stopped.

The children went outside.

"Look! What is that?" asked Mrs. Halsey.

"A rainbow!" the children cried.

The rainbow stretched across the sky.

It was very big.

After recess Andrew
sat down in his chair.
He got out his crayons
and worked at the table.
At show-and-tell time Andrew
showed his drawing to the class.

VERY NICE,
SUSAN.

"Look! Look at my rainbow!" he said.

"It's like all the color days at once!"